SHADOW FLYERS

ARIKPO LAWRENCE OMINI

Imprint:

©2019 by Arikpo Lawrence Omini

Cover-Design & setting:
Angelika Fleckenstein; spotsrock.de

Printed and published by
tredition GmbH
Halenreie 40-44
22359 Hamburg

ISBN:
978-3-7497-1851-1 (Paperback)
978-3-7497-1852-8 (Hardcover)
978-3-7497-1853-5   (e-Book)

Bibliographic information published by the Deutsche Nationalbibliothek (German National Library):

The Deutsche Nationalbibliothek (German National Library) has recorded this publication in the Deutsche Nationalbibliografie (German National Bibliography); detailed bibliographic data are available through the Internet at http://dnb.d-nb.de.

DEDICATION

This book, titled; "THE SHADOW FLYERS" is dedicated first of all to God almighty, to my family far and near, my friends and to all people of the world

INTRODUCTION

CHAPTER ONE

CHAPTER TWO

CHAPTER THREE

CHAPTER FOUR

CHAPTER FIVE

CHAPTER SIX

Supernatural, Action Adventure and Mythology

LEOPARD KING

Arikpo Lawrence Omini

A special boy is led down from the skies. An Ashanti king is born. The one prophecied to change the course of the world and time itself. The leopard king Kwakwu fled after his Kingdom was attacked and his father killed in an odyssey that will eventually prepare him for his future. He returned after completing his thirteen labours in the jungle assigned to him by Selene, Moon Goddess that cursed him with the fabled seventy-two skins of invincibility and great power.

GERMANY HAS FALLEN

n a world bedevilled by wars, hunger, inequality, social injustice, racial discrimination and intolerance, almost all of the world's rich societies such as America, the European Union, Australia and Asia set up immigration barriers in order to keep migrants and refugees from coming through their borders and seeking a new and better life, different from the one they knew before, but migrants aren't deterred. They still travel to those countries' frontiers, defying warnings, hoping to make it. In recent years, Germany has taken in many foreign migrants who fled violence, persecution, hunger and death amid a growing atmosphere of resentment, xenophobia, racism and bigotry partly ushered in by the coming to power of the United States of America's dystopian demagogue Hurricane Donald Trump, who endorses politics of hate, ethnic prejudice and religion mostly because these minorities don't look like him. Some of these people pass through hardships into the Sahara Desert. Some are raped while others are used as guinea pigs as their lives are uprooted for transactional purposes. Some are sold and forced into labor while others are killed. Those who survive the ordeal into the Mediterranean Sea lose their lives in unseaworthy boats. What's the end game to this whole global crisis? Will the world cooperate to resolve global issues besieging the world and tackle the forces that enthrone them? Should we still believe in the hope offered the world by the Fall of Berlin Wall, or, should we, in these strange times, believe the Wall has gone right back up?

tredition, 2018
978-3-7469-7963-2 (Paperback)
978-3-7469-7964-9 (Hardcover)
978-3-7469-7965-6 (e-Book)

FSC
www.fsc.org

MIX

Papier | Fördert
gute Waldnutzung

FSC® C083411

Zeitfracht Medien GmbH
Ferdinand-Jühlke-Straße 7
99095 Erfurt, Deutschland
produktsicherheit@kolibri360.de